Space Junk, Meteorites and Comets

Nicolas Brasch

Australia • Brazil • Japan • Korea • Mexico • Singapore • Spain • United Kingdom • United States

Space Junk, Meteorites and Comets

Fast Forward
Gold Level 21

Text: Nicolas Brasch
Editor: Cameron Macintosh
Design: Stella Vassiliou
Series design: James Lowe
Production controller: Seona Galbally
Photo research: Michelle Cottrill
Audio recordings: Juliet Hill, Picture Start
Spoken by: Matthew King and Abbe Holmes
Reprint: Jennifer Foo

Acknowledgements
The author and publisher would like to acknowledge permission to reproduce material from the following sources: Photographs by AAP Image/Patrick Horton, p 12 top; Corbis/ Roger Ressmeyer, p 16/ Science and Society Picture Library/ NASA, p 10; Digital Stock, pp 3, 8, 12 bottom; Michael Farmer/ Dhofar 1180, p 17 top; NASA/JPL/USGS, p 14; Photolibrary, p 5/ Ann Cutting, p 4/ Astrofoto, pp 22-23/ David Parker, back cover, p 18/ ESA, p 7/ Gerard F Fritz, p 17 bottom/ Joe Tucciarone, front cover, p 1/ Photo Researchers, p 9/ SPL/ Ronald Royer, p 20/ SPL/ Detlev Van Ravenswaay, p 15/ SPL/ Royal Greenwich Observatory, p 21 top/ SPL/ Chris Butler, p 6/The Bridgeman Art Library, p 21 bottom.

ISBN 978 0 17 012679 3
ISBN 978 0 17 012669 4 (set)

Cengage Learning Australia
Level 7, 80 Dorcas Street
South Melbourne, Victoria Australia 3205
Phone: 1300 790 853

Cengage Learning New Zealand
Unit 4B Rosedale Office Park
331 Rosedale Road, Albany, North Shore NZ 0632
Phone: 0508 635 766

For learning solutions, visit cengage.com.au

Printed in Australia by Ligare Pty Ltd
6 7 8 9 10 11 12 21 20 19 18 17

THE UNIVERSITY OF MELBOURNE

Evaluated in independent research by staff from the Department of Language, Literacy and Arts Education at the University of Melbourne.

Space Junk, Meteorites and Comets

Nicolas Brasch

Contents

Chapter 1

THE CROWDED SKIES

From Earth, the sky appears calm.
During the day, the Sun shines down.
At night, the Moon and the stars shine and twinkle.
Everything appears calm and serene.

But in reality, there are millions of objects hurtling through the skies.
These objects include space junk, **meteors** and comets.

Chapter 2

SPACE JUNK

From Earth to Space

Space junk is the term given to objects that start life on Earth but end up in space. It is believed that there are more than one million pieces of junk in space, although most of them are small enough to fit into a person's hand.

Some types of space junk are items that have been thrown away by astronauts, such as plastic bags and drinking cups.

Other common types of space junk are rocket parts that have been designed to come apart from the main rocket during a mission.

Space junk can also include pieces of equipment that have come off spacecraft and **satellites**.

Common Items of Space Junk:

- old spacecraft parts
- nuts and bolts
- solar cells
- old satellites
- bits of paint
- used rocket stages
- pieces of solid fuel

Speeding Through Space

Space junk doesn't float through space. It speeds through space at about 28000 kilometres an hour. Space junk can be a threat to spacecraft and satellites.

If a speeding piece of metal
the size of a tennis ball hit a spacecraft,
the impact would be the same
as if someone had **detonated** 25 sticks of dynamite
inside the spacecraft.

Running Words 212

Re-entry

Every year, hundreds of pieces of space junk fall back into the Earth's **atmosphere**.

Most of them are so small that they burn up before they reach the Earth's surface.

Those that do hit the Earth usually land in water, because almost three-quarters of the Earth's surface is water.

a piece of the Skylab satellite that landed in the Australian desert

Most people on Earth live close to other people, so there are vast areas of land where few people live. Even when space junk slams into the land, it usually falls nowhere near areas where people live.

Skylab

The most famous piece of space junk to fall to Earth was the USA space station Skylab.
On 11 July 1979, Skylab re-entered the Earth's atmosphere.
It broke up into many pieces that landed in remote areas of Australia and in the Indian Ocean off the Western Australian coast.

a piece of Skylab that landed in South Australia

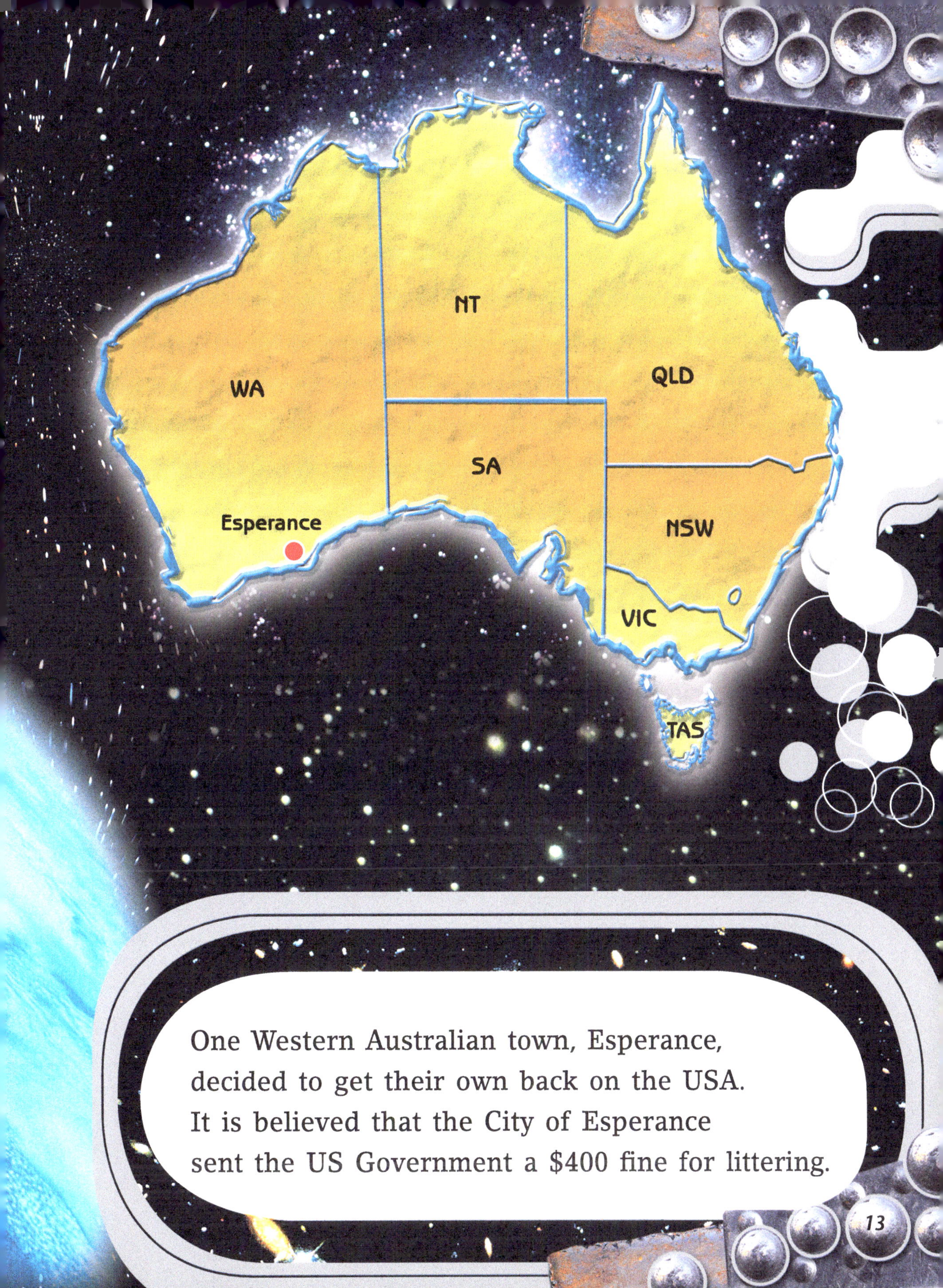

One Western Australian town, Esperance, decided to get their own back on the USA. It is believed that the City of Esperance sent the US Government a $400 fine for littering.

Chapter 3

METEORITES

Meteorites are pieces of space rocks, planets or other space bodies that fall to Earth. Some meteorites are pieces of comets. A few meteorites have been proven to be pieces of the Moon or Mars. Most meteorites come from asteroids.

Asteroid Ida, which goes around the Sun

Asteroids are very large rocks that travel through space.
asteroids
Earth
Mars
Jupiter
Most of the asteroids in our solar system are between Mars and Jupiter.

Studying Meteorites

Meteorites have provided scientists with a lot of information about our solar system. Scientists are very interested in finding out what metals are in meteorites.

This information provides them with clues about the types of life that may have existed on other planets.

Scientists who have studied meteorites from the Moon have worked out that
the Earth and the Moon were most likely part of the same planet,
billions of years ago.

meteorite from the Moon

Damaging the Earth

Meteors enter the Earth's atmosphere every day. Most are so small that they burn up before hitting the surface.

However, large meteorites have caused a great deal of damage.

meteorite crater in Arizona, USA

There have been several times in the history of the Earth that meteorites have caused so much damage that humans may not have been able to survive. It is believed that a meteorite caused the dinosaurs to become extinct.

Chapter 4

COMETS

Comets are bodies of frozen gases, ice and dust that hurtle through space. These gases, ice and dust were left over when planets and stars were formed.

Halley's Comet, 1986

Comets only become visible from Earth when they pass near the Sun.
The most famous comet is Halley's Comet.
It is visible from Earth about every 76 years, and last appeared in 1986.

Halley's Comet, 1910

Halley's Comet, 1066

The Nucleus, Coma and Tail

There are three main parts to a comet – the nucleus, the coma and the tail.

The nucleus is a small, solid part made up of frozen gases and water.

The coma is a huge cloud of dust and gases that surrounds the nucleus.

The tail is made up of tiny particles of dust that have been propelled from the nucleus by escaping gases.
The tail of a comet is usually several million kilometres long.

Glossary

atmosphere the gases that surround the Earth, or other planet

detonated exploded

meteorites meteors that have landed on Earth

meteors objects from space that burn up as they enter the Earth's atmosphere

satellites machines that orbit the Earth, often used for telecommunications

Index